ELEPANTS

Written by Joshua George

Illustrated by Jennie Poh

Licensed exclusively to Top That Publishing Ltd
Tide Mill Way, Woodbridge, Suffolk, IP12 1AP, UK
www.topthatpublishing.com
Copyright © 2015 Tide Mill Media
All rights reserved
4 6 8 9 7 5 3
Manufactured in China

ISBN 978-1-78445-428-9

A catalogue record for this book is available from the British Library

For Mum, whose pants are very impressive.

Ellie was the **biggest** girl in town,

She pushed the other girls around.

She told them where to go and when,

(Not really like a proper friend).

Mouse said, 'Does it have to be this way?
Must we always do just what **you** say?'

Ellie snorted, stomped, shook one ear,

'Hang on!'

she said, 'I thought it's clear.

I am the leader, not by chance,
Look at my wondrous ELEPANTS!

They're big, and shiny, and bright blue!
(I have a red pair for weekends too.)

I have the **biggest** pants in town ...

That's why **I** boss you all around!'

At that the animals all started speaking,

mooing,

HOOTING,

But then came a noise from by the lake,
So loud it made the jungle SHAKE!

'**Uh-oh**,' said Mouse, 'what could it be?
There's something moving through the trees ...'

Then - suddenly - a terrible '**roar!**'

'I think that it's ...
the **PANTOSAUR!**'

'It's worse,' groaned Ellie, 'I know that noise,
We should have tidied up our toys!'

Out of the trees crashed Ellie's mother,
In enormous pants of brilliant colour!

'I have the **biggest pants** of all,' she said,
'So listen up, it's time for bed!'

And so Ellie learned that it was true ...
Someone's always got bigger pants than you!